PINEY WOODS

MOOSE-MOUSE'S HOUSE

THE FISHING STREAM

SHADEY GLEN

SWEET MEADOW

HOME OF THE ORCHARD MICE

UNCLE EZRA'S SECRET PROJECT

THE APPLE ORCHARD

BIZZY & EZRA'S HOME

OLD STONE WALL

For my mother who makes beautiful quilts
and my father who tends the meadows,
both in the state of Maine.
J. B. M.


For my mother and Christina.
S. O.

# BIZZY BONES
## AND THE
## LOST QUILT

Library of Congress Cataloging-in-Publication Data  Martin,
Jacqueline Briggs. Bizzy Bones and the lost quilt. Summary:
When Bizzy loses the quilt he needs to go to sleep, Uncle Ezra
and the orchard mice try to make him a new one. [1. Mice—
Fiction. 2. Quilts—Fiction. Lost and found possessions—
Fiction] I. Ormai, Stella, ill. II. Title.
PZ7.M363165Bh   1988        [E]         87-13577
ISBN 0-688-07407-3    ISBN 0-688-07408-1 (lib. bdg.)

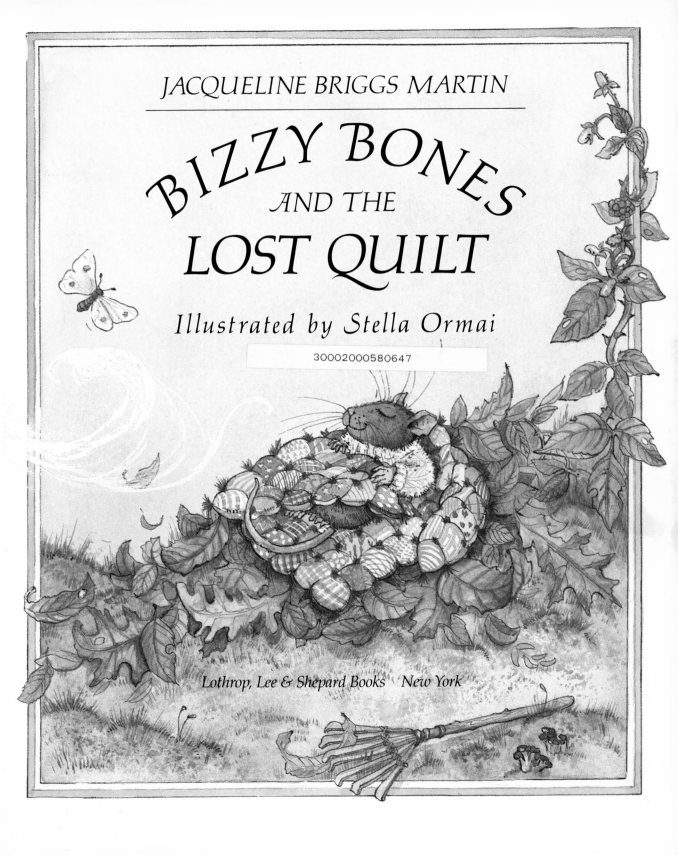

JACQUELINE BRIGGS MARTIN

# BIZZY BONES
## AND THE
## LOST QUILT

### Illustrated by Stella Ormai

Lothrop, Lee & Shepard Books   New York

One fall morning
Bizzy Bones and Uncle Ezra
went to the far edge of the meadow
to bring back seeds and nuts for winter.
Bizzy took his quilt
and rode in Uncle Ezra's wheelbarrow.

Uncle Ezra always said
Bizzy would be glad to sleep on a rock pile
or ride a wheelbarrow to Aroostook County
if he had his quilt.
Bizzy's quilt was his good friend.
He knew its every square.
He and Uncle Ezra had even made up stories
about the best ones.

Uncle Ezra worked long hours filling buckets and boxes.
Bizzy helped for a while.
Then he threw rocks into the stream
and stayed away from bumblebees.

That night Bizzy could not find his quilt.
He and Uncle Ezra searched their work shoe home
from roof to toe.

"I won't be able to sleep," said Bizzy.
The quilt was soft,
and it smelled a little like Uncle Ezra's pipe.
It filled in the extra spaces on Bizzy's bed
and gave him good dreams.

Uncle Ezra said,
"I'll give you this soft yellow blanket."
But the blanket made Bizzy's bed too warm,
and it smelled like paint thinner.

Uncle Ezra said,
"I'll give you my wool jacket. It will be just right."
But it was too small to be a good cover.
And Uncle Ezra was too tired
to think of any jacket stories.

Finally he said, "Bizzy, you'd better sleep in my bed.
We'll look for your quilt tomorrow."
And he gave Bizzy an old necktie to hold.
That night Bizzy dreamed it was winter
and he was sitting in a treetop wrapped in a cabbage leaf.

In the morning he felt cold and lonely.
Uncle Ezra said, "Let's have some breakfast, Bizzy.
Then we'll go back to the meadow and look for your quilt."

They looked in the vines, under the leaf piles,
and in the trees, but didn't find a clue.
Then Bizzy noticed a familiar red scrap
stuck in a bush by the stream.
"The quilt must have floated away," said Uncle Ezra.
"Maybe the Brambles have stopped it."
But the thorns had caught only weeds and old leaves.
Bizzy wanted to keep looking, but Uncle Ezra said,
"It's getting late. Let's ask the orchard mice.
Perhaps they found it."

The orchard mice liked to pick up things
that others left behind.
They were savers, swappers, and traders—
cousins who lived in an old suitcase
they had got for a dozen jars of jam.

"Have you seen a soft puffy quilt
that's full of color?" Bizzy asked.
"No quilts, but we have lots of rugs," said Scooter.
"We're leaving tomorrow to find what we find
and swap our old for a sackful of new," said Steptoe.
"We'll watch for a soft bright quilt," said Rufus.

Bizzy and Uncle Ezra headed for home.
Bizzy was so sad he walked straight into a Canada thistle.
Uncle Ezra pulled out the sharp prickles and said,
"I think we can make you a new quilt."
"It won't be like my old quilt," said Bizzy.
"It won't have stories. It could be anybody's."
"We can begin with the piece you found," said Uncle Ezra,
"and use some of our favorite old shirts."
Bizzy spent another night in Uncle Ezra's bed.
And he dreamed fish were keeping warm under his quilt.

The next day Bizzy and Uncle Ezra
began to cut old clothes into patches.
Uncle Ezra said,
"These pieces will make a nice warm quilt.
Just right for you."
Bizzy thought Uncle Ezra should have known
only one quilt was just right, and it was lost.

At lunch Uncle Ezra said,
"This is just like a puzzle, Bizzy.
But it doesn't fit together."
All afternoon he trimmed and stitched, stretched and tugged.
At last he said, "We may have to nail these pieces together
and fill in the spaces with birch bark.
But let's quit for now."

That night Bizzy dreamed about quilts
made out of scrap wood and splinters.
And in the morning the orchard mice brought bad news.
"We found no soft bright quilt," said Scooter.
"Just one marble, a couple of combs, and an old rag."
"Not enough to hurry home with," said Steptoe.
"Would you like to try out our new marble?"
"I have to work on this cover for Bizzy," said Uncle Ezra.
"Winter is coming, and I can't make the pieces go together."
"Maybe we can help," said Rufus.
"Steptoe thinks we could fit the peelings back onto potatoes."

While Uncle Ezra talked to the orchard mice,
Bizzy leaned against the traders' sack.
He was sure this strange quilt would have stiff corners
and smell worse than hard-boiled eggs.
He thought he was the saddest mouse
he had ever known.
Large tears dripped off his face.

He looked for something to wipe them away
and pulled on the red cloth
that was poking out of the sack.

"Where did you get this?" he shouted.
"That old rag?" said Scooter.
"A peddler found it in the stream early one morning.
She gave us the whole thing for one dandelion seed."

"It's my quilt!" said Bizzy, wrapping it around himself.
"There's a big hole in the middle," said Steptoe.
"It wouldn't keep you warm," said Uncle Ezra.
"But maybe we could fix that hole."
"Sure as strawberries," said Rufus.
"We'll fit a new quilt into that space.
We'll use the pieces you already have,
and we'll need a few more."

Bizzy was so happy he jumped up and down.
Then he picked out the shirts.
Uncle Ezra cut them into small pieces.

Steptoe and Scooter stitched them together
to make bigger pieces.
Rufus fitted the new patchwork into the old quilt.
And they all laughed and ate seeds.

They worked very late,
and when they had finished
Uncle Ezra gave the orchard mice a large basket of nuts.
Bizzy gave them his necktie and his best pine cones.

Then Uncle Ezra tucked Bizzy into his own bed.
His new quilt smelled like trout water and sweet smoke.
Bizzy missed the old colors and the old stories,
but the new patch tree was beautiful
and the old corners felt just right.
Bizzy knew his quilt
would give him good dreams
all winter long.

And whenever he found a lost button, a shiny rock,
or a scrap of cloth,
he saved it for the orchard mice.
They often stopped by to eat seeds,
show off their latest trades and fancy work,
and help patch together stories to go with the new quilt.

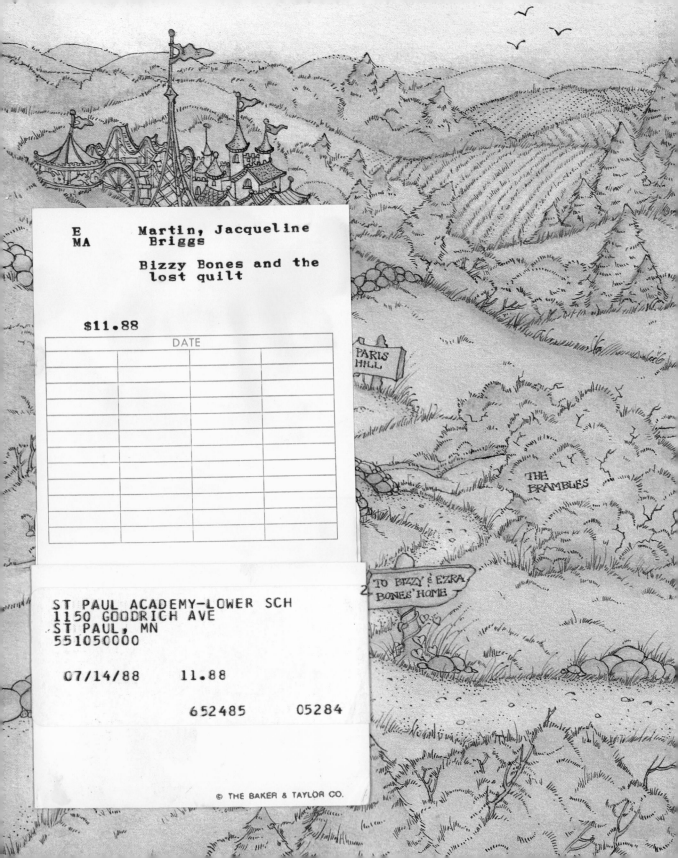

E
MA

Martin, Jacqueline
Briggs

Bizzy Bones and the
lost quilt

$11.88

| DATE | | | |
|---|---|---|---|
| | | | |
| | | | |
| | | | |
| | | | |
| | | | |
| | | | |
| | | | |
| | | | |
| | | | |
| | | | |
| | | | |
| | | | |

ST PAUL ACADEMY-LOWER SCH
1150 GOODRICH AVE
ST PAUL, MN
551050000

07/14/88        11.88

                652485        05284

© THE BAKER & TAYLOR CO.